# TO THE BIG TOP

## JILL ESBAUM

### PICTURES BY DAVID GORDON

FARRAR STRAUS GIROUX / NEW YORK

For Jensen, Carter, Dylan, and Reed
—J.E.

For Susan
—D.G.

Text copyright © 2008 by Jill Esbaum
Pictures copyright © 2008 by David Gordon
All rights reserved
Distributed in Canada by Douglas & McIntyre Ltd.
Printed and bound in China by South China Printing Co. Ltd.
Designed by Nancy Goldenberg
First edition, 2008
1  3  5  7  9  10  8  6  4  2

www.fsgkidsbooks.com

Library of Congress Cataloging-in-Publication Data
Esbaum, Jill.
    To the big top / Jill Esbaum ; pictures by David Gordon.— 1st ed.
        p.   cm.
    Summary: When the circus comes to the small town of Willow Grove in
the early 1900s, best friends Benny and Sam enjoy an exciting day helping
set up the tent, admiring the various animals, and anticipating the big show.
    ISBN-13: 978-0-374-39934-4
    ISBN-10: 0-374-39934-4
    [1. Circus—Fiction.   2. Best friends—Fiction.   3. Friendship—Fiction.]
I. Gordon, David, ill.   II. Title.

PZ7.E74458 To 2008
[E]—dc22

                                                            2006053530

## AUTHOR'S NOTE

In the early 1900s, before automobiles, radios, or telephones, before many towns had electricity, a circus visit was the highlight of the year.

From the moment a circus train pulled into a town, noise and excitement filled the air. The first section of train arrived before dawn. Workers spilled from its cars, and roustabouts and razorbacks (from "Raise your backs!") immediately set to work, rolling more than a hundred colorful wagons down steel ramps at the back of the train. Other train sections arrived soon after, holding tons of canvas, rigging, poles, and seating planks; hundreds of animals; and everything needed to construct a tent city entirely dependent upon itself. Larger circuses had blacksmith shops, cooking/dining tents, a barbershop tent, a mailman, and even their own police and fire departments. At one point the Ringling Brothers Circus employed one thousand people of vast cultural diversity, who lived together in cramped quarters and thrived despite a dizzying schedule.

While hundreds of men scurried to set huge poles and raise tents, others, including performers, dived into the tasks necessary to prepare animals and equipment for the 11 a.m. street parade and 1 p.m. show. After the show, employees immediately set to work tearing down and packing up. By dark, the circus train was chugging away, en route to another town, where the entire process would be repeated at sunrise.

My friend Sam and I were up early that morning, racing for the rail yard before the roosters knew what was what. A long *wooooooo* broke the quiet.

"It's here!" Sam hollered. "Hurry, Benny!"

I passed him. "You hurry!"

My pa said a circus had more excitement than you could shake a stick at, lots of it free for the looking.

Good thing, because Sam and I didn't have two cents to rub together.

At the rail yard, songs and shouts filled the air as men with muscles like melons raised steel ramps and lowered fancy wagons to the ground. Some hauled wood and fat rolls of canvas from the train.

The men unrolled the canvas pieces. Laced them together. Hooked them to horses and elephants.

Up went the tents! Then—*ting ting ting*—men pounded stakes into the clay.

One caught us gawking. "Know where I can find me a couple of strong boys to help with the elephants?"

"Right here, mister!" I puffed up my chest, trying to look a mite less skinny.

We lugged water till our shoulders ached. Then the man had us fork a mountain of hay. When we were done, he flipped us each a nickel!

"Not enough for the Big Top show," said Sam. "But I'll find *some*thing to buy."

"I'm buying a candied apple," I said. Just the thought of it made my mouth water. I hadn't tasted a candied apple since I was a tadpole.

Before we could find a snack wagon, another man snagged us. In two shakes, he had us carrying boards into the biggest tent for people to sit on. It was heavy work, and it took a long time. We didn't care.

"We're helping set up the Big Top, Sam," I said. "This is the best day ever."

"Couldn't get better," said Sam.

But it did.

The Big Top boss called us over. He held out two tickets. "For the show," he said.

I was so bumfuzzled I couldn't unwind my tongue.

"Better skedaddle," said the boss. "It's going on eleven o'clock. You don't want to miss the parade."

"Thank you, mister," Sam remembered to say.

We tore off like greased lightning . . .

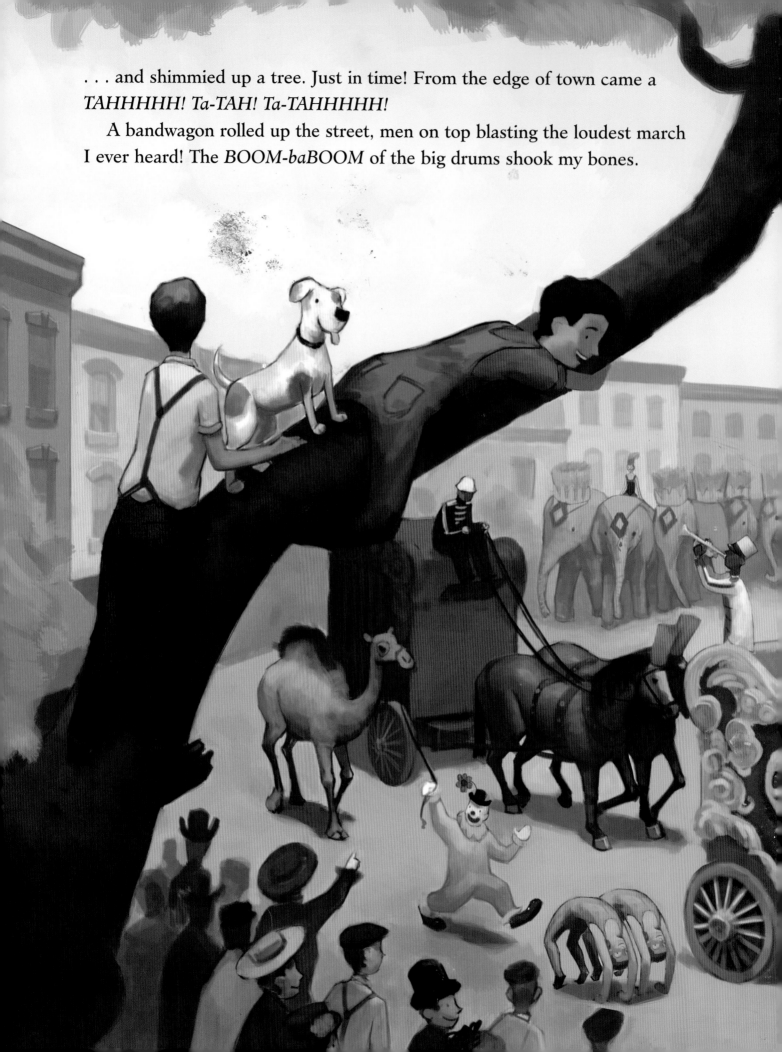

. . . and shimmied up a tree. Just in time! From the edge of town came a *TAHHHHH! Ta-TAH! Ta-TAHHHHH!*

A bandwagon rolled up the street, men on top blasting the loudest march I ever heard! The *BOOM-baBOOM* of the big drums shook my bones.

Acrobats leaped and flip-flopped. Clowns kept the crowd laughing. The parade went on and on. There was so much to see, a body needed six eyes to take it all in.

A yawning hippo in a sloshing pool! Camels and zebras! Down the street, a bear and a tiger!

"Man alive, Sam" was all I could say. "Man alive."

Finally, a whole line of elephants swayed up Main Street, their feet scraping along like sandpaper. The last one had no more than passed our tree when every head turned at a new sound. "The calliope!" some kid yelled.

That calliope's happy toots and whistles tugged at my insides somehow.
The whole crowd pushed into the street to chase after it. Sam and I were in
the lead.

"This is the best day ever!" I said.

"Couldn't get better!" said Sam.

But it did.

We moseyed down the midway, our eyes popping at the pictures painted on tents.

"A calf with two heads?" Sam scoffed. "I don't believe that."

"You just never know," I told him.

A man in a snazzy suit shouted, "Step right up! Only five cents to see the Dog-Faced Boy!"

"Benny," Sam said, pulling me back. "We both got five cents . . ."

That dog-faced boy was a sight, all right, according to his picture. But I only had the one nickel. "Nope," I said. "I'm getting a candied apple, and that's that."

"I'm buying a souvenir," Sam said, digging for his nickel. "You know, to help me remember the whole shebang."

I didn't need anything to help me remember. But I sure wished I could see the snake enchantress!

Sam pulled my arm. "Souvenirs are right there, by the red snack wagon," he said. "Mmmmm, what smells so good?"

At last, I traded my nickel for a candied apple.

"Forget the souvenir," Sam said. "Think I'll buy some popcorn."

"You can eat popcorn anytime," I said.

He passed the bag under my nose. "Not *circus* popcorn."

The smell of that popcorn got my stomach grumbling, but I was aiming to save my apple for the show.

"Could I have a bite of your popcorn?" I asked Sam. "Just one?"

"Nope," he said. "Shoulda bought your own."

We drifted into the menagerie. At first we had to hold our noses, but after a while the smell didn't seem so bad. We oohed at the giraffe. Laughed when the bear sat up. And we jumped—along with everybody else—when the tiger let out a roar.

"Your ticket's peeking from your pocket," I told Sam. "Better hang on to it." He pushed it in a bit, then ran over to a monkey in a cage.

"Look, Benny, he wants your apple!" Sam grabbed the apple and waved it just out of the monkey's reach. The monkey rattled the cage bars and screeched. Sam screeched back.

I took my apple from Sam. "Ain't nice to tease him. Now he's mad."

"So what?" Sam said. "C'mon, if you wanna get good seats."

"Bye, monkey," I said.

We were almost at the ticket taker when Sam spun around. "What in tarnation—?" He felt deeper in one pocket, then in the other. "My ticket!" he said. "It's gone!"

Gone? My hand shot into my own pocket. *Whew.* "I still got mine."

Sam was beside himself. "You wouldn't go in without me, would you, Benny?"

I was sorely tempted. Who knew when—or if—another circus would come to Willow Grove. Besides, Sam had been stingy with that popcorn and mean to the monkey. But he looked ready to bawl, and anyway, he wasn't always so bad.

"Come on," I said. "It has to be here someplace."
We pushed back through the crowd, our eyes on the trampled sawdust.
Sam's ticket wasn't by the tiger. Or the bear. It wasn't by the giraffe, either.

Then the monkey rattled his cage and screeched.
"My ticket!" Sam yelled. "Give it back!"
The monkey just screeched some more.

All of a sudden, I had an idea.

I stepped closer to the cage and took a slow bite of my apple.

"Mmmmm, this is *goooood*." I wasn't lying. That candied apple was the best thing I'd ever tasted.

The monkey eyed it hungrily.

"Wanna trade?" I asked him.

He stuck one arm through the bars, reaching . . . reaching . . .

And I took that ticket right back.

"Ho-ho!" Sam hollered. "You outsmarted him, Benny!"

"Reckon I did." I felt proud . . . for about nine seconds.

"Wait . . . What are you . . . *No, Benny!*"

"Yes, Sam," I said, handing over the candied apple. "It's only fair."

Sam kicked at the sawdust. He had cost me my apple, and he knew it. Somehow, that made losing my treat less painful.

"Come on, Sam," I said. "Let's go."

"We're about to see the Big Top show," I told Sam as we found seats.
"Can you believe it?"

"Thanks, Benny," he said. "This is the best day ever."

Clowns ran in! Music blared! The crowd cheered so loud!

Then Sam gave me some popcorn.

"Couldn't get better!" I shouted.

But it did.